JAKE
IN SPACE
MERCURY RISING

D0348093

For Samara.

First published in the UK in 2018
by New Frontier Publishing Europe Ltd
93 Harbord Street, London SW6 6PN
www.newfrontierpublishing.co.uk

ISBN: 978-1-912076-69-7

Text copyright © Candice Lemon-Scott 2015
Illustrations copyright © New Frontier Publishing 2015
Illustrations by Celeste Hulme
The rights of Candice Lemon-Scott to be identified as the author and
Celeste Hulme to be identified as the illustrator of this work have been asserted.

A CIP catalogue record for this book is available from
the British Library.

Printed in China
10 9 8 7 6 5 4 3 2 1

JAKE IN SPACE
MERCURY RISING

Candice Lemon-Scott
Illustrated by Celeste Hulme

‘Move it over to the left. Now back a bit. A bit more to the left. That's it.'

Jake shook his head as he looked up to see his mum and dad move the megascope for the twentieth time that morning. The planets were going to align in just six hours. Jake knew it would look spectacular but, really, how many times could you move a megascope in one tiny room?

'Actually, I think it needs to be a bit more to

1

the right,' Jake's mum said.

As Jake's dad started to move the megascope yet again Jake heard something land on the roof.

'Are you expecting someone?' Jake's mum asked his dad.

'No,' he replied. 'Go and check who that is, will you, Jake?'

Jake dragged himself away from his real reality computer game and made his way to the top landing. He peered through the airlock chamber and gasped.

It was the new Space 4045 super jet car with double boosters. But what was one of those doing on his roof? Someone must have the wrong address. The hatch opened and out stepped Henry. Jake couldn't believe his cyborg friend was driving the 4045! Henry had all the luck. Henry walked towards the airlock chamber. Jake opened the door to let him in.

'Where did you get that space car from?' Jake cried, not even saying hello.

'The CIA gave it to me,' Henry said matter-of-factly. 'There is even better news. The CIA said you can all accompany me to Mercury to watch the planetary alignment take place. Skye, Milly and Rory are already on board.'

Jake frowned. It sounded a little too good to be true. Why would the CIA give them their best new car to go see the planets align? Even though Henry worked for the Central Intergalactic Agency it didn't make any sense that they would give him the latest and best car in the solar system. He told Henry he suspected it was really another CIA mission they were being sent on by the agents Bree and Will.

'Of course it is not!' Henry coughed, then fake-laughed. 'It is your delayed gift.'

That was right! Jake remembered the CIA agents had promised them something special to thank them for capturing the evil Valerie and saving the Floating Hotel of Venus. This must be their reward.

Before Jake could say anything else his mum yelled out from downstairs, and asked who he was talking to.

'It's just Henry, Mum,' he called back. 'He said I can go with him to Mercury to see the planets align.'

It didn't take Jake long to convince his parents to let him go with Henry. The minute he said it was a 'good learning opportunity', they couldn't say no. The bad part was that he knew they would have loved to go too. As he left they were still trying to decide the best spot to put the megascope for viewing the alignment.

4

When he climbed on board the 4045, his friends were waiting, just as Henry had said.

'How exciting is this?' Milly squealed.

'We'll be able to see all the planets from Mercury,' Skye added.

'It's going to be amazing,' Rory said, grinning.

'Wow!' Jake exclaimed, looking around inside the car.

'Who wants to help drive it?' Henry said simply.

Jake couldn't wait to help and he was the first to leap into the front navigation seat. Skye took up her usual position at rear navigation, Milly sat by the controls and Rory put himself in the co-pilot seat.

Soon they were zipping towards Mercury at super speed. Jake looked at the projection screen in amazement. They flew so quickly that the stars they passed looked like long silvery trails. Then, as they zoomed between Venus and Mercury, an alarm sounded through the car.

'What's that?' Rory yelled.

Jake looked in the forward projection screen.

'Oh no! Asteroid shower, dead ahead.' He knew asteroids didn't appear in this zone very often but they were very dangerous when they did.

Jake turned to Milly at the control panel. 'Ah, you'd better put this racer into slow mode,' he said. One strike from an asteroid would be enough to destroy a space car, even one as powerful as the 4045.

'Wait!' Henry cried from the driver's seat. 'There is no need for slowing down. You will ruin the fun of being in a 4045.'

'But we could be hit by an asteroid,' Rory argued.

'Yeah, even with my navigation skills we

need to take it slowly,' Jake agreed.

'Full speed ahead,' Henry insisted.

'Henry, they're right,' Skye said softly. 'You know better than any of us that we'll be pulverised if we hit an asteroid, especially at this speed.'

Jake looked at his screen again. They had nearly reached the first asteroids. 'You have to slow down. NOW!'

Milly went to override Henry's command and reduce speed when Henry reached out and stopped her.

'Let go!' Milly said, looking nervous.

'We are *not* slowing down,' Henry insisted. 'Jake, tell me when the first asteroid is close.'

'What?' Rory cried. 'You're not even going to try to steer around it?'

Henry ignored Rory. 'When I give the signal, I want you to press that purple button,' he said to Milly.

Milly just frowned and held a shaking hand over the purple button.

'Trust me,' Henry said. 'When have I ever crashed?'

'Try Remedial Space Car Driving School,' Rory said.

He does have a point, Jake thought. Henry had crash-landed before, even if it was only to hide the fact he was really a cyborg working for the CIA and not an ordinary driving student.

'That was technically not a crash since the emergency braking system came on in time,' Henry reminded them, 'Plus, I know what I am doing.'

Jake had been so busy arguing with Henry he didn't see that an asteroid was directly in front of them. It looked like they had no choice but to give Henry's crazy plan a go.

'Asteroid dead ahead.'

'Hit the button!' Henry said quickly.

8

With no time to think, Milly pressed the purple button. There was a huge boom and Jake felt the car shudder. Had they hit the asteroid? He looked at the screen. The asteroid had completely disappeared.

'What was that?' Jake cried. He turned to Henry who was looking very smug.

'Asteroid-zapping lasers,' Henry replied. 'All 4045s are fitted with them.'

'You could have mentioned that earlier,' Rory growled.

'It was worth it to see your reaction,' Henry laughed.

Rory leaned in to Henry angrily but then another asteroid was in front of them.

'Asteroid!' Jake screamed.

'Hit the button!' Henry ordered again.

Milly pressed the button, vaporising the rock with the laser. Even Rory couldn't help but smile.

'Let me have a turn,' Rory said.

Henry moved aside so Rory could have a go at driving. It seemed Henry was forgiven.

They zoomed through space, zapping any asteroids that got in the way. It was like playing a real reality computer game, only this really *was* real. Rory pulled out a packet of space jubes, their favourite flight-time snack. The jubes started floating about the cabin as soon as he opened the bag. The friends released their seatbelts, hovering around to catch the jubes. Henry reached into his suit pocket. He pulled out a rubbery hand that was as big as his own.

'What's that?' Jake asked.

'You'll see,' Henry said.

He held the hand by the wrist and threw it forwards as Rory was about to catch a jube in his mouth. The wrist stretched out until it became a long cord, turning almost completely see-through. The strange material kept on stretching until it reached its target. Jake saw the target was the jubes, as the hand snapped onto one of them. Henry flicked the hand back in and the cord retracted into almost nothing. The cyborg popped the jube into his mouth.

'What *is* that thing?' Jake laughed.

'This is a super sticky hand just developed by the CIA,' Henry said, grinning. 'I have been given the test run. It seems to work correctly.'

He flicked the hand back and forth, snapping up more of the jubes.

'Hey! That's not fair,' Rory grumbled.

Henry grinned and snatched up the last jube. Rory strapped himself back into the pilot's seat, sulking over his lost snacks.

Before Jake knew it they were coming up to Mercury. It wasn't just because he had been having so much fun that he'd hardly noticed the time. It was also because the 4045 space car was the fastest car he'd ever been in – by far.

Jake zoomed in on the image of Mercury on the projection screen. It was one of the most uninteresting planets to look at. It reminded Jake a lot of the Moon with its grey surface covered in craters. The planet hadn't been much use to anyone until someone discovered the rich iron beneath the surface. It had been mined until it was almost all gone. Now no-one visited the planet anymore. At least it was going to be the best place in the solar system to view the planetary alignment. Being the closest planet to the Sun they were going to be able to see the whole row of planets when the event took place in just five hours.

Henry drove towards Mercury's exosphere. 'Milly, there is a black button to your left,' he said. 'Please press it now.'

Milly did as Henry instructed. Jake watched as a shield went around the car.

'What is that?' he asked.

'It is a heat shield to protect the car from the high temperature on the planet,' he said. 'You will be needing these too.'

Henry reached under their chairs and pulled out five specially designed space suits. They were made up of shiny silver hexagons, joined together like a quilt. As he pulled the suits out of their vacuum-sealed bags the hexagons puffed up, looking like little pillows.

'This car has everything,' Milly said, impressed.

The girls quickly slipped their suits on and then Jake put on his. Rory picked up his suit. He poked his finger into one of the hexagon shapes. As soon as he pulled his finger out the hexagon puffed up again.

'I'm not wearing that!' he said. 'It's ugly.'

'Okay, feel free to melt instead,' Henry said.

'He's right! Mercury can get as hot as Venus. You'll need a special suit on if you don't want to fry,' Skye said. Milly and Skye lived on Venus, so they knew how hot it could be.

Rory grumbled and put the suit on.

'Rory, if you will continue driving please,' Henry said.

Before he could answer, Henry floated over to the back of the car. Jake twisted around in his seat to see what he was doing. Henry opened up the control panel in his arm. The panel seemed to have all its usual buttons and dials. Then Henry pressed a tiny button in the

15

corner and the panel popped open, revealing a secret compartment. He looked like a human toolbox. The compartment had all kinds of tiny gadgets and gizmos inside it.

'What's all that, Henry?' Jake asked.

The others turned to look.

Henry pointed to the various parts on his arm. 'Tweezers, torch, whistle, blowtorch … yes, here it is.'

Jake suddenly had a sinking feeling, like he was being pushed deep underwater. Whatever the gadgets were for, he guessed they weren't going to see the planetary alignment after all. This looked a lot like something they would need for a mission. He couldn't help but feel disappointed about missing the special event.

Henry finally pulled out a round object, as small as a pea. He started walking around the car, moving it up and down.

'What are you doing, Henry?' Skye asked.

'Just testing my detector,' he replied.

'Your detector for what?' she said.

'Now is probably a good time to reveal … oh, never mind. You will all find out soon enough.'

This doesn't sound good, Jake thought. Henry's reveals always meant something bad was going on.

'Reveal what, Henry?' Skye asked, trying to speak calmly.

'Okay! There is the small matter of bombs,' Henry stated.

'Bombs?' Milly shrieked.

'Yes, four have been planted on Mercury. We have to find them and deactivate them.'

'Or what?' Jake dared to ask.

'Or when the planets align, Mercury will be sent out of orbit, colliding with Earth and destroying both planets.'

'What about Venus?' Milly said, looking

terrified. 'It's in the way of Earth.'

'Venus will be okay. It will be slightly off-centre during the alignment.'

Skye and Milly sighed in relief but when they looked at Jake's stunned face they stopped. According to Henry, Jake's home planet was seriously under threat.

'You don't think you should have told us this earlier?' Jake yelled. 'Like before we agreed to come on this trip with you?'

'I was sworn to secrecy.'

'Let me guess. By the CIA?' Skye said.

Henry nodded. 'Yes, they have received this information. But they do not know where the bombs are located.'

Jake thought immediately of his friends and family back on the space station above Earth. He felt sick at the thought of his home planet being destroyed.

'Henry! What if we don't find the bombs?

We need to warn everyone on Earth.'

'We will find them,' he said.

'What if we don't, or what if we can't deactivate them?' Jake insisted.

'We will,' Henry said confidently. He continued scanning the car with his detector, not seeming to notice that four people were staring at him angrily.

'Good! It is functioning correctly,' he said. 'You may enter Mercury's exosphere and we can begin the search.'

No-one moved for a few seconds. Then, one by one, they seemed to realise they had no other choice but to go along with Henry.

Milly shifted the car into a vertical position and Rory swung them towards the surface of the planet. Within minutes, Jake's excitement at seeing the planets align had vanished. Now he was more scared than he'd been at Remedial Space Car Driving School when Gradock was trying to destroy Earth. His heart raced faster than a car with super boosters. If Henry was right and they *did* find bombs it would be all up to them to stop them from going off.

They flew back and forth across Mercury's surface for hours with not even a single blip from Henry's bomb detector. Jake started to think the CIA had it wrong and there were none to be found after all. He liked the idea of not having to go in and deactivate something that could blow up his home planet.

'We've searched the whole planet, Henry,' Jake said. 'We're not going to find anything. I think the CIA has it wrong.'

'The CIA is never wrong,' Henry snapped.

'Jake's right,' Skye added. 'There's nothing here. You'd better call the agency and let them know.'

Henry grumbled but finally agreed he'd

contact the CIA once they found somewhere to land. Jake brought up the front screen. He could see a big, flat area that looked like the perfect landing space. He pointed it out to Rory and he nodded. They got ready to come in to land. Jake just hoped that when the mission was aborted they'd still get to see the planets align.

It looked like it was going to be an easy landing. The ground in front of the car looked smooth, not covered in craters like the rest of the area. Jake navigated Rory in and he eased them down for landing. The car slid along the surface, coming to a final stop. Everyone unbuckled their belts and got up to stretch. Jake was moving his head from side to side, his neck stiff, when he was thrown forward. Milly screamed.

'What's happening?' she cried.

Jake looked in the projection screen. The

ground had collapsed under them.

'The car's sliding into a hole!' he cried.

Henry shoved Rory aside and leaped back into the driver's seat.

'Put it in reverse,' he cried to Milly.

She quickly switched the car over. Henry moved the car backwards. There was another thump and this time Jake was thrown back.

'What's happening?' he cried.

Skye brought up the rear projection screen.

'Oh no! The ground behind us, it's ...' she began.

Before she could say anything else the ground gave way and Jake felt the car falling.

3

They landed with a heavy thump. Jake looked at the front projection screen. All he could see was dust. They seemed to have fallen into some kind of hole. He guessed it was a crater that had been covered by dirt.

'Is there anything out the back?' Jake asked Skye.

'It's hard to see,' she said. 'Wait! I can see some kind of a tunnel. There are iron beams

23

holding up the roof. We've fallen into an old mine.'

'What do we do now?' Milly asked.

'I guess we figure out how we're going to get out of here,' Jake said.

'Look!' Henry cried.

They all turned. Henry had pulled something out of his pocket. He was holding up the detector. A dull blue light was shining from it and it was beeping softly.

'It appears there is a bomb nearby. It must be underground. Inside these tunnels.'

Jake had never felt as disappointed about finding something as he did then. He'd really hoped that the CIA had got it wrong and there weren't any bombs after all. He knew the next thing to do though was try to find them.

'How are we going to get the car through these tunnels?' Milly said.

They stared at the projection screens. As

powerful as the car was, it still wasn't designed for driving through small underground spaces.

'I think we're going to have to walk,' Skye replied.

'Negative,' Henry said from the back of the car.

'What's that supposed to mean?' Rory asked.

'Let me show you. If you will please take up your positions again.'

The four took their seats, with Henry still in the driver's position. Jake hoped Henry wasn't planning to somehow force their way through with the lasers. The whole tunnel could collapse on them if he did that.

'Milly, if you will now press the yellow button on your right.'

Milly frowned but did as Henry said. Jake heard a whirring sound. He looked at the front screen. A flap had opened up at the front of the car.

'Now, press the orange one underneath it,' Henry said.

Milly followed his instructions. This time Jake saw something cone-shaped come out of the front of the car. It looked a bit like a giant corkscrew.

'And the red one under the orange button, Milly,' Henry said.

This time Jake heard what was happening before he saw it. The giant corkscrew was turning. He realised it was a gigantic drilling attachment. This car really was the best.

'Last of all, the brown button at the very bottom of the panel,' Henry said.

When Milly pressed the brown button Jake saw bright yellow light start streaming from the front of the car, like a huge torch had just been switched on. Now they would even be

able to see where they were going as they went deeper into the tunnels.

Soon they were moving forward through the tunnel. The drill in front of the car shifted rock away as they squeezed through, guided by the beeping coming from Henry's detector. Jake indicated the turns up ahead as the tunnels weaved along beneath the surface of Mercury. They seemed to be going further downwards too as they made their way towards the planet's core. The colour of the rocks started to change as the car drilled deeper.

Before long Henry's detector was shining bright blue as it beeped loudly. He held it up.

'We are getting close!' Henry said.

It was getting darker and the detector was flashing brighter as they continued on, and Jake knew they were getting closer to finding the bomb. He wished he was back up on the surface where it was safe.

Then the tunnel narrowed suddenly. Even with the car's drill, Jake could see they would never make it through. The way ahead was barely wider than a person and just as low. They were so close but now it seemed like they weren't going to make it.

The giant corkscrew tried to push through the rock. The car started to smoke and sputter.

'Milly! Emergency stop button!' Henry yelled.

But it was too late. Before Milly had a chance to hit the button, the lights snapped off and the car shut down.

Milly screamed. Skye grabbed onto Jake's arm. They were in the dark somewhere inside Mercury with no car. And there was a bomb nearby. Jake wished he was back home waiting for the alignment with his parents.

'W-w-what now?' Milly stammered.

'We will have to walk from here,' Henry said calmly.

Jake's stomach felt mushier than a bowl of freeze-dried cereal. He was so afraid of going through the tunnel in the dark. There was no other choice though. They had to find that bomb before it went off.

They cautiously stepped out of the car. Jake stretched his arms out in front of him, not knowing what he'd find in the darkness. Henry pulled a torch from the collection of gadgets in his arm and switched it on. It was only small so there wasn't much light but at least they could get an idea of where the tunnels led.

'There's the entrance,' Skye murmured as Henry held the light on the narrow opening.

Rory glanced around nervously. Milly shakily took a step forward in the darkness.

Jake swallowed hard and they started moving slowly through the tunnel.

Jake followed behind Henry, who used his bomb detector to search for the explosives set to destroy Earth. It was slow going in their bulky silver space suits. As they moved deeper into the old underground mine it got darker until all Jake could see was the thin ray of light shining from the torch and the blue light on Henry's detector. The beeping was still loud so Jake knew they were going the right way. He just hoped Henry was able to disable the bomb easily when they found it. The tunnel made him feel nervous. He couldn't wait to get out. Then he hit something hard.

'Ouch!' he cried.

'Sorry,' Henry replied.

Jake had crashed into Henry. The cyborg had stopped suddenly and Jake hadn't seen him in the dark.

'This is the spot,' Henry said, turning to the right-hand wall of the tunnel.

His detector was beeping loudly and the flashing blue light had turned indigo. The only problem was that Jake couldn't see anything. They were looking at a plain wall.

The five of them checked over the entire wall in the semi-darkness but still they couldn't see anything.

'There's nothing there,' Jake cried.

'Maybe it's buried in the wall?' Skye suggested.

'Wait!' Milly said, looking up. 'Is that it?'

Jake looked to where she was pointing. A dusty red cylinder, a bit like a big birthday candle, was poking out. He reached up and grabbed hold of it.

'No! Don't touch it!' Skye said. 'That's not a bomb – that's a rock blaster. It was probably left here when the mine was closed. If you pull it out –'

But Jake already had the red object in his hand. It started to feel warm. He knew that he'd accidentally set it off.

'Uh-oh!' he screamed. 'Run!'

Jake threw the blaster forward as hard as he could. The others turned and ran back down the mine tunnel. Jake followed last.

Boom! The blaster went off. Jake fell to the ground, pieces of dirt firing at his back as he was thrown down the tunnel with the force of the explosion.

He stayed still until the dirt settled, then rolled over and pulled his head out of the wall where it had been planted. His back stung and he couldn't see anything at all. He wiped the dirt from his face. That was better. Henry's torch was still working and now at least he could just see the pile of rubble in front of him. He looked around.

'Is everyone okay?'

'I think so,' Skye said, pulling herself up.

'Yes, but I'm so dirty,' Milly said, 'and I feel like I've eaten a grit sandwich.' She spat dust out of her mouth.

'I can't feel my leg,' Rory cried.

'There is something under me. It is wriggling,' Henry said.

'That's because you're sitting on my leg!' Rory yelled. 'No wonder I can't feel it, you great lump of metal.' He pushed the cyborg off him.

'Oh, I am sorry!' Henry said.

'Great detecting,' Rory complained. 'You could have got us all killed.'

'It is not my error,' Henry said. 'Detectors will pick up any explosive material.'

'I'm sorry I set it off,' Jake mumbled, sheepishly brushing himself down.

'Don't worry, I would have done the same,' said Milly. 'But what do we do now?'

'Head back to the car and get out of here,' Rory said firmly.

'But the mission ...' Henry began.

Everyone ignored the cyborg. They'd all had enough of explosions for one day and it looked as though the bombs weren't there after all. Even if they were, the other end of the tunnel had been blocked off by rubble from the explosion. The only way to go was back in the direction they'd come from. Jake was about to lead the way to the car when he heard a scratching sound. It was coming from the rubble.

'What? Who –' Skye began.

They walked towards the sound and through the haze of dust Jake saw a drill come through the rock, making a hole. When an opening had been made the drilling stopped and the drill disappeared. In its place a familiar shape appeared. The face poking out from the gap in the rubble was one Jake had hoped he'd never see again. The crystal smile and mushroom-shaped head were unmistakeable.

It was Gradock!

Gradock – the former triple-ace pilot who had taught Jake and his friends remedial driving. The man with the secret plot to destroy Earth.

Gradock's big hands grasped pieces of rock as he forced his way through the hole he had made. Jake noticed Henry quickly slip the detector back inside the control panel in his arm.

'Well, well, well!' Gradock snarled. 'Who do we have here?'

Jake remembered seeing that expression on Gradock's face when he was about to send the Moon crashing into Earth – until Jake and his friends had stopped him. But what was he doing here?

'I ... I thought you were in jail,' Jake stammered.

'Didn't your little cyborg friend explain?' Gradock said. 'I escaped three weeks ago. With a little help from my friend here.'

Jake couldn't believe who stepped out through the dust next. It was Valerie. On their last mission she'd tried to blow up the Floating Hotel of Venus to run a hotel of her own. Jake and his friends had stopped her too. Now both of the villains were free. But how had they escaped? And why had they teamed up?

'And now the bombs are ready to detonate to send this pathetic planet hurtling towards Earth. Even better, now that you lot have appeared we get to blow you up along with these nasty planets.'

Valerie and Gradock started laughing until Milly surprised everyone by hurling a piece of exploded rock at the two of them. Skye copied and so did Rory and Jake until they were all aiming at Gradock and Valerie. But the two just dodged the incoming rocks and swatted away the ones that reached them like they were just bits of fluff. It stopped them coming closer but it didn't exactly have them running away either. There was only one thing left to do.

'To the car!' Jake yelled.

The five ran back towards the 4045 space

car, weaving through the dim tunnels. Henry led the way, with the girls and Rory behind him, and Jake at the back. He could hear Gradock and Valerie following behind. They were so close that the sound of their puffing echoed through the old mine and up towards the surface.

Finally Jake saw the silver glimmer of the car up ahead. When they reached it Henry wrenched open the hatch and jumped inside. Milly, Skye and Rory followed, then it was Jake's turn. As he went to jump he felt Gradock's hand grab the back of his space suit. Jake reached forward. Rory grabbed his hands and pulled him safely out of Gradock's clutches. Jake slammed the hatch closed behind him.

They could hear Gradock's fists beating on the door. Jake gulped nervously as Milly took to the controls. Would the car still work after it had fallen into the mine? She went to start the engine but it just made a small whining sound. Gradock's banging was getting stronger and Jake didn't know what they'd do if he got in now.

But as Milly worked at the controls the engine finally started up. With Henry in the driver's seat they shot backwards. They reversed through the tunnels until they reached the crater where they had fallen into the mine. Milly shifted the car to vertical and they sped back up and out of the mine.

Jake had never been happier to see the surface of a planet – any planet – in his life.

5

Once they had escaped the mine, Milly set the car to horizontal as they drifted across the planet. Safely away, Rory jumped out of his seat. He stared at Henry, arms crossed angrily across his chest. 'You knew Gradock and Valerie had escaped?' he accused Henry.

'No, I thought they were still imprisoned. I only knew about the bombs,' Henry said, frowning. 'But now we know they are the ones who placed them.'

'If they've already planted the bombs, why are they still here?' Jake asked.

'Maybe they haven't attached the detonators yet?' Skye suggested.

'That must be it. There is not much time left before the alignment,' Henry said.

'They had some trouble with the detonators, I bet,' Jake said.

'Um, guys,' Skye interrupted, looking through the rear projection screen. 'We've got company.'

Jake twisted around to see the screen. Skye was right. There was a space car coming in behind them. It was pretty easy to guess who was on board.

'Move over Henry, I'm driving this time.' Rory cried.

'Wait! I have a better idea,' Jake said.

'You have a better idea than getting out of

here as quick as we can?' Rory asked.

'Yes! What if we let them catch us?' Jake explained.

'I think you breathed in too much rock dust down in that mine,' Rory replied.

'If we let them catch us we have a chance of stopping them from detonating the bombs. If we fly off we'll never find the bombs in those mines. Then Earth, and Mercury, could be destroyed.'

Rory clamped his mouth closed. Everyone was quiet. Jake hoped they'd see being captured was the only way to stop them.

'Whatever we decide, we'd better do it soon,' Skye said. 'They're on our tail.'

'Let's vote on it,' Milly suggested.

Jake's hand went up instantly. He was sure he was right but no-one else moved. He held his breath and waited. Skye's arm started to shift from her side. She put it up in the air.

'Jake's right,' she said. 'We're the only ones who can save Earth.'

After that, Milly's hand shot up.

'Henry?' Jake asked.

'Yes, I believe it is the best option,' he said.

'Then put your hand up,' Jake said.

'Oh. What a strange thing to do. Okay then,' he said, lifting his arm stiffly.

'Why do I always get outvoted?' Rory shrugged and slowly lifted his hand too.

Now Jake just had to come up with the next stage of his plan. He guessed for now they just had to think about being caught.

'Okay, keep the speed up,' Jake said. 'We don't want them to know we're trying to get caught.'

Milly set the speed control and Rory drove as though he was trying to head away from Mercury.

'That's working,' Skye said. 'They're gaining on us. Now they're flying above us. I think they're going to try to lock on.'

Just as she said it, Jake heard a clunking noise.

'I think they've just done it,' he said.

The communication screen started to crackle. Valerie's face appeared. At the Floating Hotel of Venus she had been a genius with computers. She must have figured out how to get into their car's system.

'You have been captured. You will be towed back to the mine where you will be dealt with by Gradock and myself.'

Valerie smiled nastily and the screen went blank. Jake gulped. He hoped he hadn't just got them into serious trouble. Everyone sat nervously as they were towed back to the mines. Jake didn't know how they were going to get out of there, or how they were going to find and disable the bombs. The only thing he did know was that the whole of planet Earth was relying on them.

Gradock and Valerie led them down endless narrow tunnels until they reached a mine shaft. They locked the five friends inside a tiny room that had once been used to store mining tools. There were still some picks and other items leaning against the rock wall. Jake had no idea how they'd escape. Even if they did, he had lost count of when they had turned left and right so he didn't know how they would find their way out anyway.

Everyone looked at Jake grumpily, as though it was all his fault they were stuck in here. In fact, it *was* his fault. They should have raced ahead like Rory had suggested. At least then they could have told the CIA where the villains were hiding.

'Knock knock! Can I come in?' Gradock called, laughing at his own joke.

Everyone ignored him. He shone a torch into their cell.

'I have some good news for you,' Gradock said, smiling, his crystal teeth shining against the torchlight.

'What?' Milly asked, eagerly.

'You're getting out of here,' Gradock said.

'Really?' Jake said, not really believing him.

'Not out of the mine of course, but out of this room. Valerie and I have a little problem. You are going to solve it for us.'

Valerie appeared from the shadows and stood in the light of the shining torch.

'Yes, you see my computer program will not allow me to set off the bombs automatically.'

'And we don't want to risk our own precious lives,' Gradock added. 'So you are going to do it for us.'

'We'll never help you!' Skye piped up.

'You don't have any choice,' Gradock sneered. 'The bombs have all been planted but we need them to be detonated. So we

47

have a special job for our friend Henry.'

Rory scowled at Henry, like he'd had something to do with it.

'I do not know what it is he is talking about,' Henry said firmly.

'But you soon will.' Gradock laughed so hard he started coughing.

Jake and his friends watched silently as Valerie attached a transmitter to the control panel in Henry's arm. Usually Henry's cyborg capabilities were helpful for cracking codes and carrying out their missions but this time Jake wished they didn't have a walking computer with them.

'How handy to have a cyborg to help out,' Valerie remarked. 'Oh, and if you try to pull this transmitter out it will make the bombs go off immediately.'

She clicked it into place, smiling as she explained that it would transmit the detonation signal at the exact moment the planets came into alignment. Gradock and Valerie might have been evil but they were also very good at planning mass destruction. It was a clever plan.

'With my computer programming skills and Gradock's driving prowess, it will be as easy as squashing a space bug between our fingers.' Valerie pressed her thumb and forefinger together for effect.

Jake squirmed. Now he could see why Valerie and Gradock had decided to work together. They each had the skills the other one needed. With Valerie programming the bombs to detonate at the right time and Gradock using his triple-ace pilot skills to fly them anywhere at lightning-fast speeds, they were a dangerous team.

'Yes, and we would have been flying out of here already if you hadn't messed up the detonator activation program,' Gradock grumbled to Valerie.

'If you had flown us here fast enough in the first place I would have had time to fix it,' Valerie argued.

'Well, at least we have Henry so everything will work out after all,' Gradock said, forcing a smile.

'Yes, and now we can begin our new life without pesky Earth people trying to stop us from doing whatever we like,' Valerie said gleefully.

'Or annoying kids,' Gradock added.

Gradock and Valerie laughed. Valerie pressed the timer on the transmitter and the countdown began at sixty minutes. She closed the panel over on Henry's arm. You couldn't even tell that Henry had a device in his arm that could destroy two planets. Jake felt sick. It seemed like there was no way out for them now. The villains were only an hour away from destroying Earth and Mercury – and Jake and his friends along with them.

'Now we can ditch this planet,' Gradock said.

'And it's time for you lot to say goodbye,' Valerie said, looking straight at Jake.

Jake watched helplessly as Valerie and Gradock disappeared back down the tunnel, leaving them locked up.

Once they were gone, Henry opened up the control panel in his arm. The timer flicked over to fifty-seven minutes. Henry frowned as he tried typing different numbers into the keypad underneath it.

'Can't you just turn the transmitter off?' Jake asked.

'I am trying to disable it but I cannot work out the code.'

Jake could have sworn that even in the dim light he saw Henry blush. Henry wasn't used to not being able to do something. They already knew that they couldn't just pull out the transmitter or it would make the bombs go off.

'Valerie is a computer programming mastermind,' Jake reassured him.

'It would seem so,' Henry agreed.

'What are we going to do if we can't stop the bombs from detonating?' Skye asked, worried. 'We need a plan.'

'But how can we even make a plan?' Milly cried. 'We can't do anything when we're locked in here.'

'That part is easy,' Henry replied.

He flicked open the secret compartment beneath the control panel in his arm and pulled out the tiny blowtorch. *Of course,* Jake thought, *the toolbox inside his arm!* The CIA must have known he'd need a few of those items when they sent him on this perilous mission. Henry switched it on and held it against the bars on the door.

In ten minutes Henry had made a gaping hole in the door and the five slipped out. There were only forty-five minutes left until the bombs would detonate.

'What do we do now?' Milly asked.

'We have to collect the bombs and throw them from the car into space,' Henry said.

'There's not enough time for that!' Skye said.

'We have to try,' Jake argued.

Henry nodded and pulled the bomb detector from the secret compartment.

The five friends bolted through the tunnels beneath Mercury's surface, following the indicator on Henry's detector. They turned in the direction of the flashing blue light and the beeping that grew louder as they headed down towards the centre of Mercury. It became darker and hotter the deeper they went but the detector showed they were getting close. Jake just hoped they were on the track of the real bombs this time, not just old explosives from the mines.

Finally the detector turned indigo and emitted one long beeping sound. Henry stopped.

Jake could just make out a long silver object on a ledge cut into the rock wall. That had to be one of the bombs. The cyborg very carefully pulled it off the ledge.

'That is one,' he said.

'How much time now?' Milly asked.

Henry handed her the bomb. She took it gingerly.

'Thirty minutes.'

'We have to hurry!' Rory yelled.

They found the other three bombs across the mid-line of the planet. Gradock and Valerie had planted them in a line. By blowing up the three bombs across Mercury's centre they'd be sure of destroying the planet by exploding it from the inside. The plan all made sense. Henry explained that when the bombs went off the planet would break in two, like an egg cracking.

With only twenty minutes remaining, the next step was to get back to the car and get themselves, and the bombs, away from Mercury before the bombs detonated.

Finding the car wasn't as easy as they'd thought, though. They'd gone through so many twists and turns locating the bombs. It was even hard to know which way was up and which was down.

'How long have we got?' Jake asked, puffing as he ran through the tunnels.

'Sixteen minutes,' Henry said.

'We're never going to find the car in time,' Rory complained.

'What if we use our suits' temperature gauges?' Skye suggested.

'What do you mean?' Jake asked.

'The surface is the coolest point, right?' Skye explained.

'Yes, so?' Rory mumbled.

'If we follow the direction of the cool air in the tunnels we'll find the surface.'

'Brilliant!' Jake said.

They all looked at the gauges on their suits. They took a left turn and ran along that tunnel.

'My gauge is going up,' Milly cried.

'We have to go the other way then,' Skye said.

They all turned and ran in the opposite direction. Jake noticed the temperature on his suit start to drop. He started to think they might just make it out in time after all.

They continued to turn in the direction of the lower temperature. Every now and then they'd have to double back when it went up instead of down. But it seemed to be working as the temperature started to drop faster. Then, up ahead, Jake saw light streaming onto the tunnel floor.

'There it is!' he exclaimed.

'How long have we got?' Milly asked.

'Nine minutes,' Henry said.

'Let's get moving!' Jake cried.

Nine minutes, he thought. Would it be long enough to get off the planet and release the bombs safely into deep space?

Jake and his friends clambered on board the 4045. Milly took her position at the control panel and started up the engines. Henry sat in the driver's seat and everyone quickly buckled themselves in.

Jake made his way to the back of the car, carrying the bombs. The plan was to put the bombs in the emergency escape pod. Once they got far enough away from Mercury, they would release the pod from the space car.

The bombs would explode safely out in the middle of space.

'How long now?' Rory asked.

'Six minutes left!' Henry announced. 'We must go!'

Milly went to start the car.

Nothing happened.

'It won't start,' she cried. She pushed buttons and turned dials but the engine was silent.

Henry unbuckled himself and came over. He tried to get the car going but it was no use.

'Milly is right. Something has been disabled,' he said, checking the control panel. 'Ah, yes. It appears the starter is missing.'

'What does that mean?' Rory asked.

'It means if we don't lift off soon, this planet is doomed – and Earth along with it,' Skye replied.

Just as she said it, Jake discovered what had happened to the starter. As he reached the

emergency escape pod he found the pod was already full. That mushroom-shaped head peering out through the pod's communication screen was unmistakable. It was Gradock! But what was he doing in there? And why wasn't he escaping the doomed planet with Valerie?

Jake looked into the camera on the outside of the pod.

'Valerie locked me in here. You'll need this,' Gradock squeaked, defeated.

He held up a small object that looked a bit like a computer stick. It was the starter.

'If you want to get out of here and stop the bombs you'll have to let me out,' Gradock threatened.

'Let him out,' Henry said.

'We can't do that!' Jake screamed.

Rory didn't look happy.

'I want to see Valerie arrested as much as you do,' Gradock barked. 'She tried to get me killed. After I helped her too.'

'I think we should let him out. We need that starter!' Milly said.

'And we need the escape pod free so we can put the bombs in it,' Skye agreed.

'Okay,' Jake agreed, 'but no funny business or we'll put you back in the escape pod and send you into space.'

Jake saw Gradock's lip curl up into a smile. He hoped they weren't making a really big mistake, but they had to get away from Mercury before it was too late.

Once the pod was opened Rory raced over and grabbed the starter. He ran back to the control panel and handed it to Henry. Meanwhile, Jake put the bombs inside the pod and locked it tight. He took his seat and buckled himself in, ready to go. There were only five minutes left until the bombs would go off.

'How do I unlock the starter?' Henry said to Gradock, turning it over in his hands.

'I don't know,' Gradock snapped. 'Valerie's probably locked it.'

'It says here how to do it,' Skye announced.

Skye had pulled out a panel under the main control centre. There were instructions encrypted on it. Jake never would have thought of looking for a driver's manual. Skye scanned the pages with her finger until she found the right part.

'Here it is!' she read. 'Unlocking the starter.'

Skye read out the instructions and Henry pressed the small buttons on the starter in sequence until its case popped open. He clicked it into the car's control panel. Milly switched on the double boosters and they were off with only three minutes to spare. Jake hoped it would be enough time to get far enough from the surface of Mercury. Henry held the timer up so he could see when to send the escape pod off while Rory drove them higher above the planet. It got down to thirty seconds, twenty, ten ...

'Release the pod,' Jake said.

Milly hit the release button and everyone gathered around the rear projection screen, holding their breath.

The pod spun out into space. As the timer on the transmitter went off there was a huge flare of white light in the distance. Three more explosions followed. It had worked. The bombs had gone off safely.

At the same time the planets came into alignment. Lined up together, they looked like a long, brilliant white star, shining at the different points with a long tail reaching down. Everyone clapped and cheered and hugged one another. Jake looked over at Gradock. He was scowling at the screen. His dream of blowing up Earth had failed yet again. Jake went over and stood beside him.

'Now would probably be a good time to tell us why Valerie locked you in the pod,' Jake said.

Gradock clamped his mouth shut and crossed his arms. He wasn't about to say anything but Jake could already guess what had happened.

'She double-crossed you, didn't she?' Jake said.

Gradock just stared straight ahead but his brow wrinkled.

'She took off and left you here to be blown up. She even thought to lock the starter to our car so you couldn't escape.'

'But how did she get someone as big as you locked in here?' Skye asked. 'She wouldn't be strong enough, would she?'

'No, she tricked me into going into the pod

65

to check it was activated,' Gradock grumbled. 'When I went into it she locked me inside.'

'That's not what a friend would do,' Milly said.

'We were never friends,' Gradock snapped. 'It was a business arrangement. She did the programming and I flew us in and out of here safely. We were both meant to go to Venus.'

As soon as he said it Gradock had realised his mistake. He'd just told them where Valerie was hiding.

'Take us there!' Jake commanded.

Gradock said nothing for a second, then nodded.

Henry moved aside and Gradock took over the driving. He told Milly to shift the car into vertical. While Gradock was focused on driving, Henry opened up the control panel in his arm and typed something in. A hologram with a message to the CIA asking for help appeared above his arm for a second, and then was gone just as quickly.

'Strap yourselves in,' Gradock said. 'We're going to have to move fast if we're going to catch her.'

Jake shouldn't have been surprised that Valerie was hiding out on Venus. He saw her abandoned castle looming in the front projection screen as Gradock drove them through the planet's atmosphere. When Jake and his friends had uncovered Valerie's plot to destroy the hotel where she worked, they discovered that she had built her own Venus hotel. It was made of obsidian rock from cooled lava flows, and she had built it with the help of her robot.

As Gradock brought the space car in to land in front of the castle, he explained that he and Valerie had planned to come back to the castle to hide until they could escape to the outer planets. He agreed to help Jake and his friends capture Valerie as long as they let him go free afterwards. Jake didn't know how Gradock and Valerie had escaped from the CIA jail but he bet there'd be extra security next time they were caught.

They went up to the front of the castle, stepping across a rock drawbridge with a lava moat flowing beneath it. Jake could smell the sulphur from the surrounding volcanoes in the air. The horrid odour just added to the feeling he had that he couldn't wait to get away from this place. He hoped the CIA arrived soon.

They stopped in front of the imposing

castle doors, which were three times the height of Gradock. Jake pushed on the doors. Nothing happened. He pushed harder. They didn't budge.

'Are you sure she's come here?' Jake asked.

'She's not going to just welcome people in, is she?' Gradock said. 'She's in hiding, remember?'

'So how do we get in?' Milly asked.

'Leave it to me,' Gradock replied.

Gradock explained that he and Valerie had a secret code combination.

'It should work,' he added. 'She probably wouldn't have changed it because she'll think I'm blown up by now.'

He told the kids to hide around the side of the entrance doors. He cackled, muttering to himself that he couldn't wait to see the look on Valerie's face when she found out he was still alive. Not knowing what else to do, they did as Gradock suggested. Jake peered around the side as Gradock entered the code on the keypad. For a while nothing happened. Just as Jake was about to step back out, there was a deep creaking sound and the door started to open. Jake and his friends raced out from the side of the castle but the door was already starting to close again as Gradock slipped inside.

'Wait!' Jake screamed.

By the time he reached the doors they had closed tight again, with Gradock safely inside. He'd tricked them. Jake looked at the keypad helplessly. He hadn't been able to see what numbers Gradock had pressed because his big mushroom head was in the way. He tried a few sets of numbers but it was no use. The keypad kept showing 'Incorrect code' so the door wouldn't open.

He turned to Henry. 'Can you crack this code?'

Henry went up to the door and started typing number combinations so fast Jake couldn't even see what he was entering. But still it was no use. The door stayed locked tight.

'What do we do now?' Milly cried.

'Maybe there's another way in,' Skye suggested.

They split up and searched the castle for another door, a window, any way in. As he felt along the rock walls Jake wondered what was going on inside the castle. Were Gradock and Valerie going into battle against each other or would they team up again to carry out their plan once and for all? Finally, they all returned to the main entrance. No-one had found an opening. It looked like these doors were the only way in.

Jake looked up into the reddish sky and wondered what they could do. Henry had

even tried his blowtorch but it was no use against the strong obsidian rock. Then he saw a sleek, silvery car appear. The CIA! He had never been so glad to see their car come into view. They would be able to arrest Gradock and Valerie and put them back in jail where they belonged.

The car came into land beside the 4045. Jake waited for the agents Bree and Will to step out. Instead, the agent who appeared was the CIA's junior agent Jake had met on their last mission. He wondered how her training was going. Last time Will had bossed her around a lot but now she was looking more confident. Her space suit was properly fitted and her CIA briefcase swung by her side. Jake and his friends raced up to greet her.

'We received Henry's distress signal,' she said. 'When we saw he was headed for Venus we knew something was going wrong with the mission.'

'Where are Bree and Will?' Jake asked, looking towards the car but not seeing anyone else exit.

'They, ah, just sent me. My first solo mission,' Junior said, smiling uncertainly. 'Don't worry, everything will be okay now.'

'But that's a bit hard, isn't it?' Skye said.

'What do you mean?' Junior asked.

'Well, Gradock and Valerie are a couple of the most evil villains ever. And they just escaped from the CIA prison!'

Junior straightened and pulled the front of her suit down tight, lifting her chin. 'I think I can handle this. And I have you to help me.'

'Of course, sorry, I –' Skye stammered.

'Where are they?' Junior interrupted.

'In there,' Jake said, pointing to the doors.

Henry quickly told her what had happened.

'Are you certain you have the skills to

complete this part of the mission?' Henry said, frowning, when he'd finished explaining.

Junior answered him by placing her briefcase on the ground. She snapped it open.

'What do you think?' she replied.

She pulled out a rope made of space worm silk, a laser beam cutter and something that looked like the X-ray goggles Jake had only heard about.

'Ah, yes,' Henry said.

Jake couldn't help but smile. He didn't usually see the cyborg lost for words.

'Right, let's go,' she said.

They all followed Junior back to the castle doors. The agent switched on the cutter and a red beam shot out from it as she pointed it at the door. In just seconds she had cut an opening in the solid door. It had made a perfect rectangle, like a door inside a door.

'After you,' she said.

Jake gulped nervously. Even though he was glad to have the agent with them, he knew how clever, and dangerous, Gradock and Valerie could be. They would be hard to catch. Unless, of course, Valerie and Gradock were fighting it out. Then they might be distracted enough for Junior to arrest them easily. Jake really didn't know what to expect.

Inside was an empty foyer. Everything was made of obsidian rock, just as Jake remembered from the last time he was here. There wasn't a single splash of colour in the place. It was black and lifeless. There wasn't any sign of Valerie, or Gradock, either.

'We will need to split up to find them,' Junior said. 'I'll go upstairs with Henry. Jake, you go to the right with Skye. Rory and Milly can go left.'

She handed them each a slim metal tube.

'This is a silent tracking whistle. When you

find them, or if you get into any trouble, blow on it. It will send me an alert you're in trouble and it will give me your location.' She pushed a small hearing bud into her ear. 'Let's go!'

Jake and Skye headed down the hallway leading off the foyer to the right. He hoped they found Valerie and Gradock quickly. The whole place gave him the creeps.

Jake and Skye crept along the dim hallway. There were doors leading off it. They cautiously opened each one and checked inside the rooms. Jake guessed they were meant to be hotel rooms but there was little more inside each room than a stone bed and a table and chairs. There was no sign of Gradock or Valerie but they weren't likely to be inside the rooms. Jake and Skye raced down the next hallway until they came to a familiar door. Jake recognised it as the entrance to the lab where Valerie had hatched her last evil plan.

'In here!' he called to Skye.

But when he opened the door to the lab there was no-one there. Worried they were running out of time to find her, they tried another hallway. Towards the end of it Jake could see it branched off left and right. *This is worse than the tunnels of Mercury*, Jake thought. It was such a maze. But at least it was only a castle – before long one of them would have to find the villains.

He knew Junior had paired them off for safety but he and Skye decided that it would be quicker if they each went a separate way. Jake gestured for Skye to go right while he went left.

As Jake ran down the hallway he noticed there were no doors in this part of the castle.

Up ahead it looked like the hall came to a dead end too. *What sort of hallway has no doors?* he thought. It was spooky. There wasn't even anything to check. Finally he got to the end and leaned against the smooth blank wall, panting. As he did, something moved. There was a door. He must have stumbled upon a secret entrance. He pushed hard against it and the wall swung open.

Stepping through, he found himself in a huge room that looked like some kind of control centre. Jake gasped. There were shelves lined with silvery rocket-shaped objects. *Oh no!* he thought. *More bombs!* Gradock and Valerie must have planned to destroy more than just Earth and Mercury. There was enough firepower here to destroy all the planets. Valerie must have come back to finish the job she thought she'd started. Jake shivered. It looked like the two evil masterminds had plotted a plan to blow up most of the solar system.

Jake tiptoed along the far wall and entered another connected room, where things got even worse. There against the wall was not one but about ten robots, exactly the same as the one Valerie had with her the last time Jake and his friends were here. The robots stood there lifelessly, like knights of armour lining a castle in medieval days. Jake wondered how it was possible the bombs and the robots had been made. According to Gradock, he and Valerie had only escaped from jail a few short weeks ago. Surely they couldn't have done all this evil work in that time.

He heard a noise. There were voices coming from a room close by. Jake quickly hid behind one of the motionless robots. It wasn't hard to figure out that the people arguing were Gradock and Valerie. Jake listened in.

'– and you thought you'd double-cross me?'

Gradock was snarling.

'I … I …' Valerie stammered.

'But you didn't do a very good job of it, did you? Those stupid kids interfered with our plans and stopped the bombs.'

'What?' Valerie screeched.

'And now I'm going to make sure that this time it's all done properly.'

Jake stepped back. He accidentally knocked one of the robots, sending it crashing to the floor. His cover was blown! In seconds Gradock was heading towards him. Jake panicked, not knowing what to do. Then he remembered the whistle Junior had given him. He turned around so his back was facing Gradock. He pulled the whistle out and blew it. Just as he had finished stuffing it back in his pocket Gradock grabbed his suit and spun him around.

'If it isn't our little friend come to visit us,'

Gradock sneered.

Jake tried to make a run for it but Gradock was too strong. He held Jake by the back of his suit and dragged him into the other room. Jake was surprised to see that Gradock had tied Valerie to a chair and she squirmed angrily when she saw Jake. Jake couldn't help but smile as he remembered how Valerie had tried that trick on him and his friends when they'd found out she was trying to destroy the Floating Hotel of Venus. Now she was getting what she deserved. His smile quickly faded though as Gradock roughly pushed him into another chair beside Valerie and tied him up too. His only hope now was that Junior had heard the whistle and would come to rescue him.

Gradock walked over to a big 3D screen. It showed the planets of the solar system revolving. There were red dots glowing in the centre of each of the planets.

'What are those spots?' Jake asked.

'You're not smart enough to guess?' Gradock said, his crystal teeth gleaming as he roared with laughter. 'The red dots mark the planets ready to be blown apart as soon as the bombs go off.'

'But that's all the planets!' Jake cried.

'So it is,' Gradock said, grinning. 'In just ten minutes our whole solar system will be gone forever.'

Jake looked at Valerie. She was even whiter than before but her neck was bright red as sweat poured down her face. It was not a good sign.

'Not here! Not Venus!' Valerie cried. 'Not my beautiful castle!'

If the situation hadn't been so awful Jake would have laughed at Valerie for calling her castle beautiful. Instead, he almost felt sorry for her.

'Now, I just have to activate the launch sequence and I'll be safely heading to the Moon while you all, um, die.' Gradock laughed again, his chin wobbling like space goop.

'Not so fast!'

Jake turned his head. Phew! It was Junior. Skye, Milly, Rory and Henry were following behind.

'You heard my whistle,' Jake sighed with relief, as Henry quickly cut Jake free from the chair.

Before Junior could say anything in reply Jake quickly went on to explain that Gradock was about to blow up the planets and escape to the Moon.

'Well then, I'll be needing this,' Junior replied.

She reached into her case and pulled out a remote control. It looked a little like the controls Jake used for his real reality computer games. Junior held it up and pressed a button on it. Jake and his friends looked at each other, confused. Just then he heard a metallic scraping sound and then footsteps. It was the robots. They came marching into the room. Junior pressed the arrows on the remote.

Jake couldn't believe it. She was controlling the robots! Jake and his friends looked at each other, surprised. Now with the robots' help it would be all over for Valerie and Gradock. They would be going back to the CIA jail as soon as the bombs were deactivated.

But to his amazement the robots didn't go over to Valerie, or Gradock. They actually walked towards Jake and his friends, forming a circle around them. Was Junior trying to protect them somehow? It seemed a weird way to do things. Still, she must know what she was doing. Junior turned to Gradock and Valerie.

'I'm very disappointed in both of you. After I freed you from jail you've repaid me by mucking up the one thing you were supposed to do.'

'What are you talking about?' Jake interrupted.

Junior frowned. 'All these two had to do was set off the first bombs but they didn't even do that. I was looking out for the CIA alert that Mercury had hit Earth but it never came. Then the CIA received a distress signal from Henry. It wasn't easy to convince Bree and Will they should let me take care of it. After all, I am just a junior agent, but luckily they agreed.'

'You're a spy?' Jake said, shocked.

'How else do you think these two idiots got out of jail? They couldn't do it themselves. I did need them to help with the bombs so I could carry out my plan though. It was going to be perfect too. Until they messed it up. Things are more difficult now that you know all about me. But never mind, none of you will be able to tell your story to the CIA because you'll all be blown into specks of space rubbish by the time the bombs go off.'

She turned back to Gradock and Valerie, walking up to them.

'Now what am I going to do with the two of you?'

10

As Junior turned, Henry silently reached into his pocket and pulled out the super sticky hand. In one smooth movement he flicked it towards the agent. It hit the remote, gripping on, and the cord retracted in a flash. Henry grabbed hold of the remote with his other hand. The CIA's annoying invention had finally been useful for something other than stealing people's jubes.

89

'I order you to give that remote back,' Junior cried.

'I do not take orders from spies,' Henry said.

It took Henry only a few seconds to work out the remote. Junior made a sudden move towards the door but Henry was too fast for her, wheeling the robots around in an instant so that the spy agent was surrounded. Valerie started screeching and trying to pull herself free from the chair but it was no use. She wasn't going anywhere. Junior was shouting at Henry, who was making the robots stamp their feet all at once. In the confusion, Jake looked around for Gradock. Where was he?

'Gradock's gone!' Jake cried.

'We have to stop him before he gets away,' Skye said.

'Henry, you hold Valerie and Junior. We'll go after Gradock,' Jake shouted over the noise.

Jake and his friends raced into the other

room. There was no sign of the villain. They ran through to the next room. There they spotted Gradock at the far end. He was grabbing the bombs off the wall.

'Stop right there!' Jake yelled.

Gradock turned and saw them. He pulled down another bomb, his arms now full, and ran out the open door, slamming it closed behind him. Jake wrenched it open and looked left and right, but already Gradock had disappeared down one of the long hallways.

'Where do you think he's gone?' Milly asked.

'He's making a run for it. He must have headed for the space cars,' Jake answered.

The friends ran in the direction of the castle's front doors. By the time they had raced over the drawbridge, Gradock had already boarded Junior's CIA car, probably thinking it would be the faster of the two.

'Quick! He's escaping,' Rory cried, running towards the car.

Gradock was too quick for them. When they had almost reached the car he gave them a crystal smile as the hatch closed, leaving them facing a blank silvery wall. Their only hope now was to catch up to Gradock in their own car.

'To the 4045,' Jake commanded.

The friends turned and headed towards it. Rory took the driver's seat, Jake took the front navigation and Skye the rear navigation. Milly started up the engines and set the boosters for maximum speed. Within seconds they had taken off and were on Gradock's tail.

'Where do you think he's going?' Milly asked.

Jake knew where he must be heading. It had been Gradock's only home since he'd been kicked off Earth and been sent to teach

92

remedial space car driving. And it was where he had his secret underground computer lab.

'He hasn't got any detonators for those bombs. I bet there's only one place he knows he can get some,' he said.

All together the others said, 'He's heading for the Moon!'

Jake zoomed in on the screen until he could see the CIA car clearly. It really must have been one of the best cars in the solar system because even with the 4045 Gradock was way ahead of them already. It didn't help that he had been a triple-ace pilot either.

'He's over a minute ahead of us,' Jake told his friends. 'Can you make it go any faster?'

'Both boosters are engaged,' Milly said.

'And I'm driving as hard as I can,' Rory added.

'It's hopeless, we'll never catch him,' Milly sighed.

'There has to be a way,' Skye said.

Jake tried to remember everything Gradock himself had taught them about driving when they were at the Remedial Space Car Driving School. It was teamwork that had got them through, and it was teamwork that had helped them stop Gradock the first time. That was the answer. There was only one of him but there were four of them. If they could race the car together they would be able to stop Gradock. Jake was sure of it.

'Gradock might be the better flyer but we've got four brains between us. How can we outwit him?' he said.

As they kept flying everyone was quiet, trying to think of something, anything, they could do to stop him. Meanwhile, the gap between Gradock and them grew larger.

'This is the most modern car ever. There has to be *something* we can do,' Skye said.

94

'That's it!' Jake cried. 'The lasers!'

'How are they going to be any help?' Milly asked.

Jake quickly explained his idea. They would have to do it right or it would be a disaster. But it could just work and right now they didn't have any other choice but to try it.

Soon the grey, crater-covered surface of the Moon came into view. Jake could see that Gradock would be coming in to land in the next few minutes. He gave the signal to Milly. She set the lasers to the lowest setting. The idea was to cause some damage, not destroy everything in their path.

'A bit more to the right,' Jake said to Rory.

Rory eased the car over.

'A little more,' he said.

Rory moved too far, and Jake instructed him to pull back a tiny bit to the left. It reminded him of his mum and dad trying to position the megascope for the planetary alignment. If only they knew what he was doing right now.

'Okay, that's it. And ... fire it, Milly!'

Milly hit the button and a laser beam shot out from the car. It headed in a straight line towards Gradock's car but he had started to come into land and had lost altitude. The laser went straight over the car, missing altogether.

They gave it another try. This time Skye worked out the exact coordinates for the angle Gradock was coming in for his landing. That way they wouldn't miss as he headed closer to the Moon. If they didn't get his car this time, he'd land and get to those detonators before they could do anything to stop him.

Jake stared through the projection screen. When they were lined up, Jake gave Milly the signal to fire. Her hand shook as she pressed the button. The laser shot out again. This time it hit Gradock's left engine, which exploded in a display of sparks like a shooting star.

'You did it!' Jake cried.

'Now we just need to get the other one,' Rory said.

Gradock had already lost some speed now one of the engines was out, and they started gaining on him quickly. It wouldn't be fast enough though if they couldn't take out the other engine. Again Skye carefully worked out the new coordinates. When she had the position, Jake guided Rory down and to the left. Again on his signal, Milly fired.

They all held their breath as the laser shot out. It was a little too far to the left but it still managed to hit the engine. The right side of Gradock's car sparked and turned black.

'Did that get him?' Milly asked.

Jake looked at the screen. At first it was hard to tell but then the car began to drift and slow right down.

'Sure did! He's lost power,' Jake said.

Now there was just the last but most dangerous part of their plan to go. They had to get Gradock to surrender.

illy flicked on the communications controls. With both cars belonging to the CIA it was easy to tune into Gradock's frequency. The microphone crackled and the video screen came on. Gradock's face appeared and he didn't look happy. His cheeks ballooned out with rage. Jake spoke into the microphone.

'It's all over, Gradock,' he said, trying to sound tough. 'Surrender now. We'll flip our car and line up with yours so you can climb in through the emergency hatch.'

'I'm not surrendering to a bunch of ex-remedial students!' Gradock spat.

'You have no choice. Without any engines you'll crash. You have to come on board our car,' Jake argued.

'Never!' Gradock shouted.

The screen went blank. Gradock had switched off his communications. Jake looked to his friends helplessly. He didn't know what else they could do if Gradock didn't want to be saved. He suddenly felt bad for destroying the engines, but couldn't think of what else they could have done.

'What do we do now?' Milly asked.

'We'd better follow him in,' Skye said.

Milly set the controls for landing and Rory flew close behind Gradock. Jake watched nervously through the projection screen.

'Okay, he's about to land,' Jake said.

The silver CIA car flew towards the surface of the Moon. With the engines gone Gradock had lost control of the car and it wobbled dangerously as it came in to land. The car hit the ground hard and spun on impact. It flipped over, sliding across the surface of the Moon until it hit a crater. Jake watched the car slip off the edge of the crater and crash down on its roof. The car lay lifelessly, like a space bug stuck on its back, smoke pouring out.

'Did he land?' Rory asked.

'Um, yeah, but he's stuck inside a crater, upside down.'

'I wonder if he's okay,' Milly said nervously.

'There's only one way to find out,' Rory said and he shifted the landing gear.

Rory's Moon landing was much smoother than Gradock's. They quickly unbuckled their belts and Jake opened the entry hatch. Milly, Rory and Skye followed behind.

They reached the shallow crater that Gradock's car had landed in. Jake peered down but he couldn't see anything because of all the smoke. He breathed in the fumes and started to cough. Waving his hand across his face, he motioned for the others to follow.

They climbed into the crater. There was still no movement coming from Gradock's car. Jake found the hatch. It was bent out of shape from the crash. He pulled on it but it wouldn't open. The others joined in but still it wouldn't move.

'We're going to have to try to get in through the emergency exit,' Jake said.

They ran around to the side of the car but it was locked from the inside.

'I've got an idea,' Skye said. She climbed out of the crater.

Jake looked at Rory but he just shrugged. Knowing Skye, whatever her idea was it was likely to work.

In a minute she reappeared, carrying a moon rock in her hand.

'Stand back everyone!' she said.

She pulled her arm back and threw the moon rock at the emergency hatch window as hard as she could. It smashed a hole big enough for her hand. She put her arm through the gap and carefully opened the window from the inside.

They slipped in through the hatch. It was quiet in the car but Jake could just hear a low moaning sound. He followed it and found Gradock slumped in the driver's seat, his head resting on the control panel. The crash had pushed his seat against the panel, pinning him in tight so he couldn't move.

'Gradock?' he said.

Gradock moaned again. 'Horrible kids,' he muttered.

'I think he's going to be okay,' Jake said.

Jake heard a roaring sound coming from outside the car.

'What's that?' Milly asked.

Skye raced out. Moments later she poked her head back in.

'It's another silver space car. I think it's the real CIA this time.'

They left Gradock and ran out to the car. The hatch opened and Bree and Will, the CIA agents, stepped out. Jake quickly led them to where Gradock was trapped.

The first thing Bree did when she got to the car was put Gradock in space cuffs. Then she pulled a saw from her briefcase and cut him free from the seat. She and Will led him to their car and secured him in the holding bay. Will pulled a space worm silk tow rope from the back of the CIA car.

As Will passed the 4045, he ran a finger along the scratched paintwork and dinted edges from when they had fallen into the mine on Mercury. He frowned as he looked at his dusty finger.

'Um, sorry about the new car,' Jake mumbled.

Will sighed. 'At least it didn't come off as badly as Gradock's.'

He climbed into the crater, attached the tow rope to the crumpled wreck of the CIA car Gradock had crashed, and clambered out again.

'How did you find us anyway?' Jake asked. 'I thought Junior got the distress signal Henry sent.'

'We always receive a copy of any signals that come through as well,' Will explained. 'It's the CIA's back-up method.'

'Lucky!' Milly said.

Will checked the tow rope was holding tight. 'We're ready to go,' he said.

Milly, Skye and Rory went back to the 4045. Minutes later they were driving all the way back to Venus with the CIA agents following behind with the captured Gradock. It wouldn't be long now and they'd be back on Venus to arrest Valerie and Junior.

Rory slid in to land on Venus, with the CIA agents gliding in next to them. Bree stepped out to greet them once more, explaining that Will would stay to keep an eye on Gradock. Meanwhile Jake and his friends would lead Bree to the control room where Henry was holding Valerie and Junior inside the robot ring.

Jake still got a shivery feeling when he entered the black castle. He wondered what would happen to it now Valerie was about to be arrested, yet again. No-one would ever want to stay in the horrible hotel, that was for sure.

Finally they made it to the control room.

To Jake's surprise, Henry was standing beside one of the robots. He had them all lined up in a row. They were taking turns at throwing the super sticky hand as far as they could.

'Forty metres,' Henry said. 'I win!'

'Henry!' Jake cried.

Henry jumped and quickly pulled the hand back in, slapping himself in the face with it. He peeled it off.

'What are you doing?' Jake groaned.

'I have finally found some others that enjoy playing sticky hand snatch. Mind you, I did have to reprogram them to make them enjoy the game.'

'What about Valerie and Junior?' Skye asked.

The two villains gingerly stepped out from between two of the robots.

'Don't worry. I made them play as well. How about another round?'

'Please, no more,' Valerie whimpered. 'I hate this game.'

'Take us away now,' Junior agreed.

Jake and his friends laughed. Henry must have been torturing them with the game for quite a while.

'I'm happy to take care of that,' Bree chuckled.

She pulled out her space cuffs and told Valerie and Junior to put their hands behind their backs. She cuffed them together and led them from the castle. Jake and his friends followed behind. Bree stopped once she reached the space car.

'Please wait here a moment,' she said.

Bree roughly led Valerie and Junior to the car. Jake sighed, glad they were back in the hands of the CIA. She came back out with Will a few moments later.

'They're all safely captured now,' Bree said.

'Your parents will be starting to worry where you are,' Will said to Jake and his friends. 'We'd better get you home fast. Come with me. Bree will drive the 4045 back to CIA Headquarters.'

Jake and his friends followed the agent and climbed into the silvery CIA car. Jake looked around as he made his way to a passenger seat. He had never seen so many gadgets and dials. There were screens all around the car showing views of space from different angles.

'Wow!' Milly breathed, sitting in one of the passenger seats. The seatbelt buckled itself across her lap.

Rory sat in a chair next to her. It buckled itself too and he was tilted back so he could see out of the top hatch. 'I want one of these,' he murmured.

Will laughed as he sat in the driver's seat.

Henry took his place next to Will. Jake and

Skye sat down last.

'Ready?' Will asked.

'Ready!' Skye grinned.

'Venus, Earth, Mars,' Will said, using voice command.

The flight path came up on the screen. In seconds they shot into the sky so fast Jake could hardly breathe. As he sucked in a breath, he wondered if there'd be another mission for them soon. He didn't know the answer to that. But he did know that he was *very* glad to be heading home right now.

ABOUT THE AUTHOR

Candice enjoys writing stories about turbo space cars, hurtling asteroids and evil villains. Her quirky style, fast-paced narratives and originality appeal to reluctant boy readers in particular.

Following several years working in the media, Candice now devotes her time to her writing and to raising her two daughters.